**LEVEL THREE**

# Tunes for
# Clarinet Technic

by
*Robert Lowry*
*in collaboration with*
*James Ployhar*

## Foreword

Level III of "Tunes for Clarinet Technic" is a continuation of the very effective and enjoyable policy of developing technical proficiency through familiar melodies of a technical nature, and with scale and rhythm variations based on well-known tunes.

Some of the melodies and variations may be challenging and at first seem difficult. In this case always work them out slowly and accurately, then gradually increase the tempo to the correct speed.

In general, the book progresses in difficulty and correlates with the Method book "Bb Clarinet Student", Level III. It may also be used in conjunction with any Clarinet Method at the Intermediate or Advanced Level.

---

The Belwin "STUDENT INSTRUMENTAL COURSE" - A course for individual and class instruction of LIKE instruments, at three levels, for all band instruments.

*EACH BOOK IS COMPLETE IN ITSELF BUT ALL BOOKS ARE CORRELATED WITH EACH OTHER*

### METHOD
### "The Bb Clarinet Student"
### For individual or Clarinet Class Instruction.

*ALTHOUGH EACH BOOK CAN BE USED SEPARATELY, IDEALLY, ALL SUPPLEMENTARY BOOKS SHOULD BE USED AS COMPANION BOOKS WITH THE METHOD*

### STUDIES & MELODIOUS ETUDES

Supplementary scales, warm-up and technical drills, musicianship studies and melody-like etudes, all carefully correlated with the method.

### TUNES FOR TECHNIC

Technical type melodies, variations, and "famous passages" from musical literature for the development of technical dexterity.

### Bb CLARINET SOLOS

Four separate correlated Solos, with piano accompaniment, selected, written or arranged by Robert Lowry:
A Festival Fantasia
. . . . . . .*Robert Lowry*
Prelude . . . . . *Armas Jarnefelt*
Melody . .*Ignace Jan Paderewski*
Lucia di Lammermoor
. . . . .*Gaelano Donizetti*

2

# Contents

NOTE: Although some of the above melodies have appeared elsewhere in the STUDENT INSTRUMENTAL
COURSE they are here presented in a more extended form or in a new and more challenging key.

B.I.C.308

## La Donna e Mobile

GUISEPPE VERDI

## The Campbells Are Coming

SCOTCH DANCE

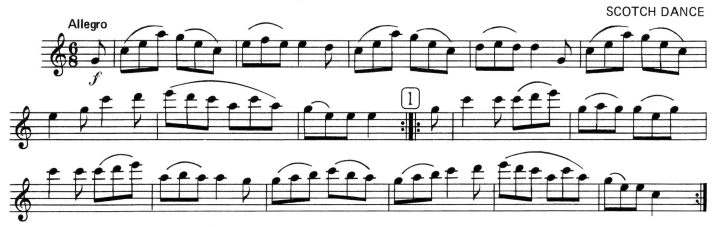

## Concerto - Finale Theme

FELIX MENDELSSOHN

B.I.C.308

# Sweet and Low

JOSEPH BARNBY

# Hail to the Chief

JAMES SANDERSON

# Funiculi, Funicula

LUIGI DENZA

# Officer of the Day

R. B. HALL

# Landlord, Fill the Flowing Bowl

ENGLISH FOLK TUNE

B.I.C.308

6

# March from "Love of Three Oranges"

SERGE PROKOFIEV

# Cielito Lindo

MEXICAN FOLK TUNE

# March of the Tin Soldiers

PETER ILYITCH TSCHAIKOWSKY

# Love's Old Sweet Song

JAMES MOLLOY

ritard

# Bouree

GEORGE HANDEL

# The Heron

HUNGARIAN FOLK TUNE

# King Cotton

JOHN PHILIP SOUSA

# Habanera from Carmen

GEORGES BIZET

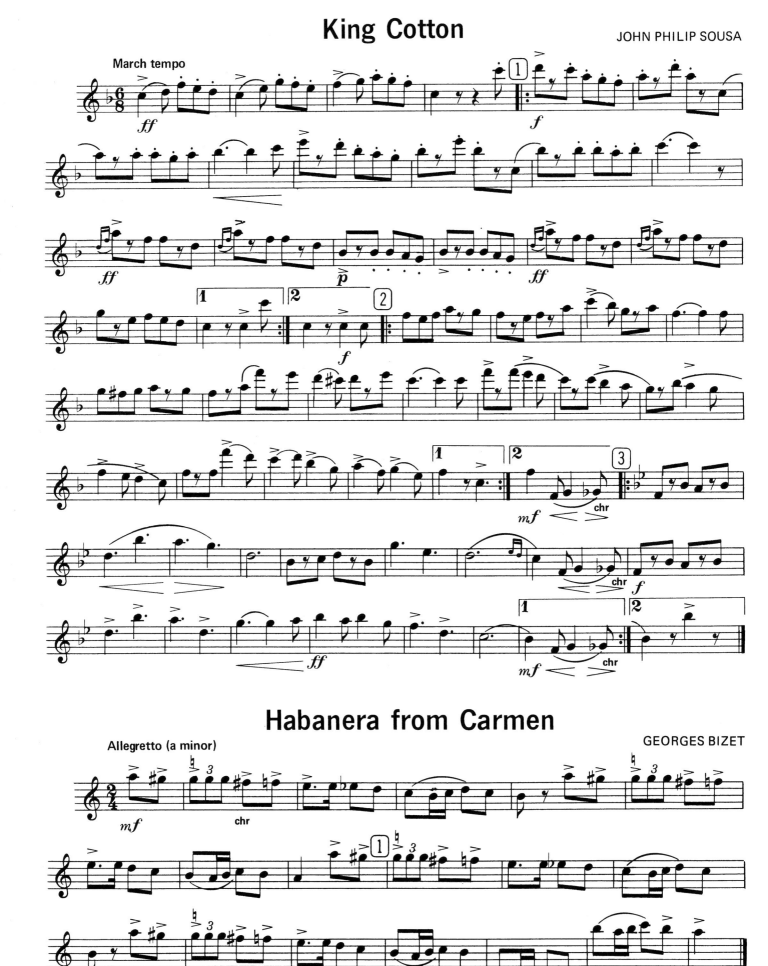

# Sonata Theme

# Irish Jig

# March of the Toys from "Babes in Toyland"

# THEME AND VARIATIONS
## Auld Lang Syne

ROBERT BURNS

THEME

# Washington Post

JOHN PHILIP SOUSA

# Minuet - Trio

LUDWIG van BEETHOVEN

12

# Turkish March

WOLFGANG MOZART

# Mattinata

RUGGIERO LEONCAVALLO

# Dance of the Reed Flutes

PETER ILYITCH TSCHAIKOWSKY

# Hail, Columbia

PHILIP PHYLE

# Santa Lucia

NEAPOLITAN BOAT SONG

# El Capitan

JOHN PHILIP SOUSA

# From the Blue Danube

JOHANN STRAUSS

*Work the rhythms out in three before trying it in one to the measure.

# THEME AND VARIATIONS
## Loch Lomond

SCOTCH AIR

# Polka from "The Bartered Bride"

FREDERICK SMETANA

# Prayer from Cavalleria Rusticana

PIETRO MASCAGNI

# La Cucaracha

MEXICAN FOLK TUNE

# Tenth Regiment

R. B. HALL

# Aragonaise

JULES MASSENET

# Kashmiri Song

AMY FINDEN

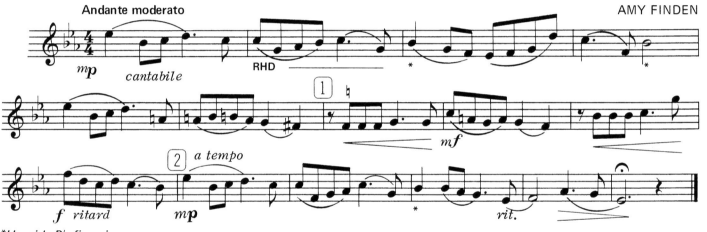

*Use side B♭ fingerings.

# Angel's Serenade

GAETANO BRAGA

# THEME AND VARIATIONS
## Blue Bells of Scotland

**THEME**

TRADITIONAL

Work out the variations slowly before playing at faster tempos.

**VARIATION I**

**VARIATION II**

# Fairest of the Fair

JOHN PHILIP SOUSA

# Mazurka

EMIL MLYNARSTI

# Humoresque

Use side B♭ fingerings unless marked otherwise.

ANTON DVORAK

# Funeral March of the Marionette

CHARLES GOUNOD

# Wiegenlied (Cradle Song)

CARL MARIA von WEBER

# Aloha Oe

HAWAIIAN TRADITIONAL

# Air

JOHANN SEBASTIAN BACH

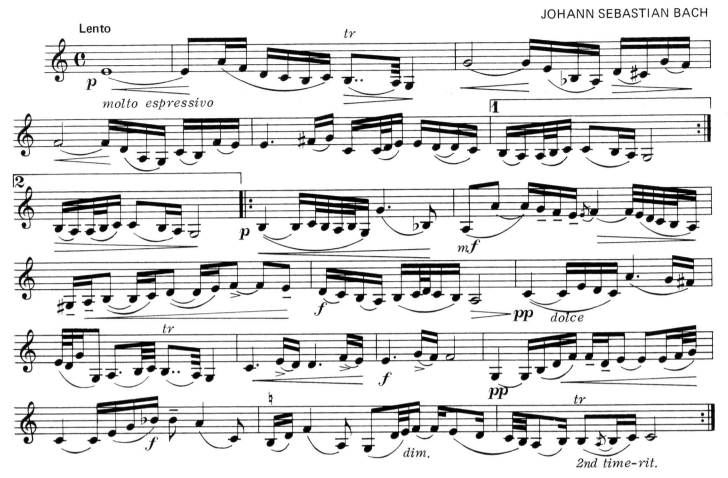

# The Hunter's Prayer

CARL MARIA von WEBER

# Fantasie Impromptu

FREDERIC CHOPIN

# March Slav

PETER ILYITCH TSCHAIKOWSKY

# El Relicario

JOSE PADILLA

B.I.C.308

# Invitation to the Dance

CARL MARIA von WEBER

# Hymn to the Sun

N. RIMSKY-KORSAKOV

## The Spanish Cavalier

WILLIAM HENDRICKSON

## Rondo in C Minor

LUDWIG van BEETHOVEN

## The Minstrel Boy

IRISH TUNE

## The Fountain

CARL BOHM

B.I.C.308

# Rakoczy March

HECTOR BERLIOZ

# The Last Rose of Summer

FRIEDRICH von FLOTOW

# Peasant Dance

FOLK TUNE

# Quintette Excerpts

WOLFGANG MOZART

# Londonerry Air

TRADITIONAL

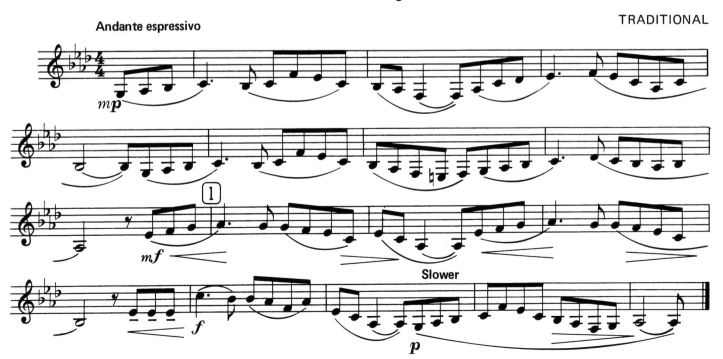

# Euryanthe Overture

CARL MARIA von WEBER

Allegro con fuoco

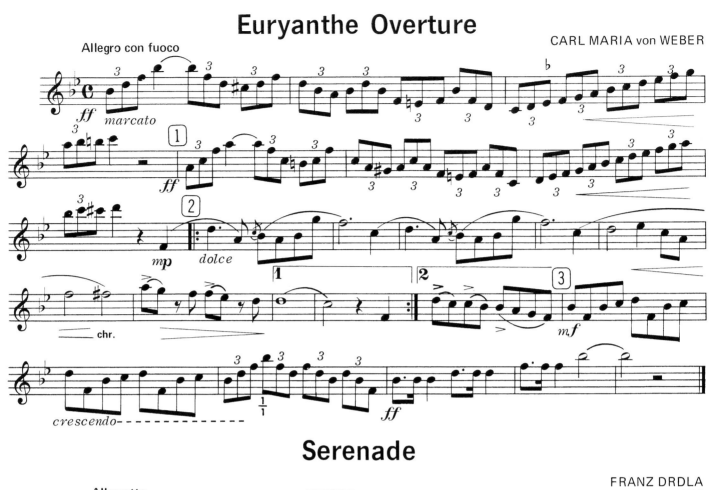

# Serenade

FRANZ DRDLA

# Poupée Valsante

(Dancing Doll)

EDWARD POLDINI

Tempo di Valse (In one)

# Killarney

**Allegro moderato**

MICHAEL BALFE

# Lucia di Lammermoor (Sextet)

GAETANO DONIZETTI

**Larghetto**

*accelerando-----------------------*

# Across the Plain

CZECHOSLOVAKIAN FOLK TUNE

**Allegro**

*Use chromatic fingerings.

B.I.C.308

# Oberon Overture

CARL MARIA von WEBER

# Walther's Prizesong

RICHARD WAGNER

# Tales from the Vienna Woods

JOHANN STRAUSS

# Czardas

V. MONTI